ABDOPUBLISHING.COM

Reinforced library bound edition published in 2016 by Spotlight,
a division of ABDO, PO Box 398166, Minneapolis, Minnesota 55439.
Spotlight produces high-quality reinforced library bound editions for
schools and libraries. Published by agreement with Marvel Characters, Inc.

Printed in the United States of America, North Mankato, Minnesota.
092015
012016

THIS BOOK CONTAINS
RECYCLED MATERIALS

marvelkids.com
© 2016 MARVEL

Elements based on Figment © Disney.

CATALOGING-IN-PUBLICATION DATA

Zub, Jim.
 Figment : journey into imagination / writer, Jim Zub ; artist, Filipe Andrade
and John Tyler Christopher. -- Reinforced library bound edition.
   p. cm. (Figment : journey into imagination)
"Marvel."
Summary: Dive into a steampunk fantasy story exploring the never-before-
revealed origin of the inventor known as Dreamfinder, and how one little
spark of inspiration created a dragon called Figment.
ISBN 978-1-61479-445-5 (vol. 1) -- ISBN 978-1-61479-446-2 (vol. 2) -- ISBN
978-1-61479-447-9 (vol. 3) -- ISBN 978-1-61479-448-6 (vol. 4) -- ISBN 978-1-
61479-449-3 (vol. 5)
1. Figment (Fictitious character)--Juvenile fiction. 2. Dragons--Juvenile
fiction. 3. Adventure and adventures--Juvenile fiction. 4. Graphic novels-
-Juvenile fiction. I. Andrade, Filipe, illustrator. II. Christopher, John Tyler,
illustrator. III. Title.
741.5--dc23
                    2015955126

Spotlight

A Division of ABDO
abdopublishing.com

Journey Into Imagination
Part Two

JIM ZUB writer
FILIPE ANDRADE artist
JEAN-FRANCOIS BEAULIEU colorist
VC'S JOE CARAMAGNA letterer

JOHN TYLER CHRISTOPHER cover artist

JIM CLARK, BRIAN CROSBY,
TOM MORRIS & JOSH SHIPLEY
walt disney imagineers

MARK BASSO assistant editor
BILL ROSEMANN editor

AXEL ALONSO editor in chief
JOE QUESADA chief creative officer
DAN BUCKLEY publisher

special thanks to
DAVID GABRIEL

FIGMENT

Imagination. Such a wonderful application of the human mind—to conjure up dreams and ideas and, if you're lucky, use them to better the world. **Blarion Mercurial,** a young inventor at the Academy Scientifica-Lucidus, has been using his to come up with an alternate energy source at the demand of his boss, **Chairman Illocrant.**

Blair's creation, the **Integrated Mesmonic Converter**, was designed to form energy out of pure thought. Its trial run blew up in his face, but Blair revised it and called forth from the deepest reaches of his mind a figment of his imagination: a purple dragon with two tiny wings, big yellow eyes, and the horns of a steer, called, appropriately enough, **Figment**.

Unable to present Figment as a valid energy source, Blair tweaked the machine again and it seems that he's opened up a portal to another world beyond even his wildest imagination.

Ah, the joy of creation.

Back at the Academy Scientifica-Lucidus, London, England.

Blair! BLAIR! You barmy madman, how do we shut this thing OFF?!

Think...think, Stuberry! There must be a solution!

Some kind of switch...maybe a button?!

KRAKOOM

By Jove, I can feel it reading my brain!

This... this madness must stop! I require ORDER!

**Early Figment and Dreamfinder character designs
for the Journey Into Imagination ride by X Atencio
Artwork courtesy of Walt Disney Imagineering Art Collection**